Yoram Gross

Blinky Bill
Remembers Nutsy's Birthday

by Sally Farrell Odgers

Illustration by
artists of Yoram Gross Film Studios
based on scenes from the ABC TV series
Blinky Bill's Extraordinary Excursion

an
ABC
BOOK

Nutsy was miserable. She wouldn't smile and she wouldn't play.
'I'm going for a walk,' she said.

'What's wrong with her?' asked Flap.

'It's her birthday,' said Blinky. 'She thinks we've forgotten. We'll have to think of a surprise.'

Unfortunately, none of them had any ideas. 'We can't even bake her a cake,' mourned Blinky. 'Nutsy's the only one who knows how to cook!'

'I'll go and find something to cheer her up!' said Flap, and he marched off into the bush.

He hadn't gone far when he tripped over a rope. 'Jumping jellybeans! A great big tent!' he exclaimed. 'What's going on?'

Just then, the owner of the tent appeared. 'I'm Captain Possum and this is my concert party! Singing, clowning, dancing! Bring your friends!'

Flap was delighted, and went back to fetch the Gang.

'It's just the thing!' agreed Blinky, but when they arrived at Captain Possum's tent, they were sadly disappointed.

'I'm afraid the show has just been cancelled,' said Captain Possum. 'My artistes are all incapacitated. Madam Melba has lost her voice, Slap and Plodge are hurt, and Donny has lost his wig. Without them there is no show.'

'We'll help,' offered Blinky. 'Dancing, singing, we can do it all! One performance only.'

While Blinky and the others worked out their acts, Captain Possum went to see his ailing artistes in the dressing room. 'You can all relax and recuperate,' he said kindly. 'I've found some replacements.'

The artistes exchanged glances of dismay.

When it came time for Nutsy's surprise, Blinky blindfolded her and led the way through the bush to the tent.

When Blinky removed the blindfold Nutsy squealed with joy, 'Oh, how exciting!'

Nutsy took her seat and Captain Possum announced the first act – Flap and Splodge!

Flap and Splodge hadn't had a lot of practice at being clowns, but the audience thought they were very funny – especially when Flap fell out of his jumbo-sized pants.

The laughter and applause sounded very loud to the artistes, still sitting in the dressing room.

'It's those little animals Captain Possum was talking to earlier!' said Slap the clown in dismay. 'They're stealing our show!'

'We'll be out of work,' warned Donny the dancing dog. 'Out of work! At my age!'

'The show must go on, and so must we!' said Plodge. He began to unwind the bandage from his foot.

Madam Melba agreed. 'Yes, darlinks, we will go on,' she said. 'We'll stop those little imposters!'

The artistes, miraculously recovered, stormed out of the dressing room.

In the concert tent, Marcia was trilling like an opera singer.

'I don't believe it!' muttered Blinky.

'Neither do I, darlink,' said Madam Melba, arriving beside him.

Just then, the glorious voice began to falter. Marcia ducked under the curtain and the voice resumed.

'Aha! So zat's the little secret!' said Madam Melba. She thrust Marcia aside and revealed – a gramophone.

'What's going on?' demanded Captain Possum.

'She's a fake!' cried Madam Melba, as she snatched up the gramophone.

'Come back here!' stormed Marcia as she chased after Madam Melba.

The audience laughed and cheered, especially when Plodge, Slap and Donny arrived.
Plodge threw a bucket of water at Marcia, but it missed and drenched Madam Melba.

Captain Possum's clowns tried to grab Marcia, but she held them off, throwing punches left, right and centre.

'They think they can push us around!' squeaked Marcia. 'Equal rights for mice!'

'Flap to the rescue!' cried Flap, and attacked with his own bucket of water.
Plodge threw a custard pie and in a moment there was total uproar as water and pics
flew all over the stage.

'I thought they were all meant to be sick!' exclaimed Captain Possum, staring at his artistes. 'I'll be ruined! I've got to get the curtain down!'

Hearing this, Blinky quickly made everyone bow as if it had been part of the act.

'You stole our show!' said Donny when the curtain came down.

'We thought you were sick!' said Splodge.

'We had to pretend to be sick, darlink,' said Madam Melba. 'We never had any rest, no days off. Captain Possum works us too hard!'

'Tell him you want a rest,' said Blinky.

'We have contracts,' said Donny gloomily. 'He could turn us out.'
'Yes – now he has you as replacements!' cried Madam Melba.
The artistes looked miserable.

'No he hasn't!' grinned Blinky. 'We told him one performance only! Now you tell Captain Possum you want new contracts, or you'll leave the show!'

The artistes did as Blinky suggested, and Captain Possum agreed. 'I don't suppose you would like to stay on as well, Blinky?' he said. 'We're about to start a big tour!'

'No thank you!' said Blinky. 'Now – let's celebrate the new contracts and Nutsy's birthday with a real party!'

And they did.

Published by ABC Books for the
AUSTRALIAN BROADCASTING CORPORATION
GPO Box 9994 Sydney NSW 2001

National Library of Australia
Cataloguing-in-Publication entry
    Odgers, Sally Farrell, 1957–
    Blinky Bill remembers Nutsy's birthday.

ISBN 0 7333 0510 5.

1. Koala – Juvenile fiction. I. Australian Broadcasting
Corporation. II. Yoram Gross Film Studio. III. Title.
IV. Title: Adventures of Blinky Bill (Television program).

A823.3

Designed by Kaye Binns-McDonald
Illustrated by Yoram Gross Film Studios
Edited by Tina McIntosh
Set in 13/14pt Cheltenham Light by Typezone, Epping NSW
Colour separations by Litho Platemakers, Adelaide
Printed and bound in Australia by Pirie Printers, ACT

7.95 – 8.5

5   4   3   2   1